Viku and the Elephant

A Story from the Forests of India

Debu Majumdar

Illustrations by Lynn Wolfe

Bo-Tree House

Published by
Bo-Tree House, LLC
1749 Del Mar Drive, Idaho Falls, ID 83404 USA

For more information about Bo-Tree House, please visit our website at
www.Botreehouse.com.
First U.S. edition 2011

Publisher's Cataloging-In-Publication Data

Majumdar, Debu [Debaprasad (Debu) Majumdar], 1941 –
Viku and the Elephant – a story from India/ words by Debu Majumdar; illustrations
by Lynn Wolfe.
1st ed.
p. cm.
Summary: A young boy and a small elephant become friends in a forest in India.
Together they defeat ivory thieves.

Copyright © 2010 Debu Majumdar
All rights reserved.

ISBN: 0983222703
ISBN 13: 9780983222705

Elephants – fiction. 2. East-Indian boy – fiction. 3. Friendship – fiction. 4. Forest –
India. 5. Animals – India. 6. India – Culture and customs. 7. India – fiction.   I. Title

[E] – dc22

Library of Congress Control Number: 2010919241

PZ7.M2586 2011

For
Rajeev and Nikhil

The author gratefully acknowledges his indebtedness to Krish Mandal, whose continuous advice and design talent have made this book possible. He also thanks Catherine Majumdar, his editor and companion in life.

Viku and the Elephant
Part 1

A long time ago, even before your parents were born, a boy named Viku lived in India at the edge of the *Shapnobahn* Forest. He was thin with dark brown skin, a round face, black hair, and eyes as dark as chocolate. He lived with his parents in a little mud hut next to the Ganges River.

The forest was big and beautiful with tropical trees, but ferocious animals lived there, and large crocodiles patrolled the river. From his hut Viku could hear the roars of tigers, but he was never afraid because he had grown up in the forest.

Every morning his parents went out in search of work. At the end of the day they bought rice, lentils, and vegetables with the money they earned that day. Sometimes they could not find work, and there would be very little to eat.

One day Viku woke up late, after his parents had already gone out. "No food anywhere," he grumbled as he looked inside the pots and tin cans in the kitchen. "Not even a single grain of rice!"

He wanted to search the high shelf, but his hands could not reach there. "I'm so hungry," he said and turned to look outside. The sun was already up over the deep green jungle.

There was no school for miles around, so Viku did not go to school. His parents had not gone to school either.

"I cannot stay hungry all day," Viku told himself. "I must find some fruit in the forest."

Just then the shrill sound of a striped hyena pierced the air. Viku remembered that his father had told him not to wander in the forest, and especially not to go far from home. But he was hungry and the forest beckoned him. He brushed his hair with his fingers and picked up his small, curved *Gurkha* knife. His thin, dark brown legs hurried toward the forest.

He searched and searched, but could not find any fruit to eat. Only tiny green mangoes hung in the trees, no ripe fruit. He kept walking and crossed several small streams. Soon he was deep in the forest. Tired and hungry, he sat down under a large *Bodhi* tree with heart-shaped leaves.

After awhile, Viku heard an elephant trumpeting and plants being smashed. He tiptoed toward the noise. Peeking through the branches, he saw a young elephant thumping the ground with his hind leg, trying to shake something loose. What was wrong with the elephant? Viku crept closer.

A snake was wrapped around the elephant's hind leg!

It was biting the elephant's backside.

Viku had never heard of a snake biting an elephant. How could this happen? Did the elephant step on the snake's tail?

He heard the elephant's sad, helpless cry, "Ouhooo! Ouhooo!"

Viku was a skilled knife-thrower. He took out his knife and hurled it at the snake. The knife hit the snake's head. The snake stopped moving and fell to the ground. The elephant turned around and tossed it away with his trunk.

Then the elephant looked at Viku. He raised his trunk high in the air and bellowed, "Ahoo! Ahoo!" That was a different cry, a cheerful sound.

The elephant walked toward him. Viku felt no fear because the elephant didn't look angry. When the elephant reached him, he bent down in front of Viku with his trunk stretched forward. Viku patted his head. The elephant did not move.

"Do you want me to climb on you?" asked Viku.

The elephant tilted his big head, as if saying, "Yes."

Viku scampered up the elephant's trunk and settled right behind his head.

The elephant walked back to the dead snake. It was eight feet long—Viku's knife still stuck in its head. Viku jumped down to get his knife. He cleaned it with fresh, green leaves. As he worked, he talked to the elephant. "You know why I came here? Because I'm hungry. When my parents don't find work, we have no money and nothing to eat. I thought I'd find something to eat in the forest."

He put the knife in his belt and saw that the elephant was quietly listening. Two small, black eyes blinked at him.

"I wish I could find something valuable to sell," Viku whispered. "Then I'd be rich. My parents wouldn't have to go out every day and look for work." He patted the elephant. "You are lucky. There's always something for you to eat in the forest."

The elephant bent down and raised Viku up with his trunk. Viku squealed with delight as he was lifted and plunked snugly behind the elephant's head. The elephant strolled deep into the forest. They went to a place where there was a path through the trees, just wide enough for elephants. Viku never knew that elephants had their own secret paths. Tall trees stood on each side, and sunlight beamed through the branches, lighting the way.

They passed a waterfall. Viku saw a few banana trees. Soon there were more. Viku had never seen so many banana trees in one place.

He realized he must be in the land of elephants because they love bananas.

The elephant stopped near a tree with a big cluster of ripe bananas hanging on one side.

"What a good elephant you are!" Viku exclaimed, and he slid down the elephant's trunk.

After they both feasted on bananas, Viku cut some for his parents. "I must go home now," he said. "My parents return home at this time. They'll worry if I'm not there."

The elephant took Viku back to the river near his home.

"How did you know where I live?" Viku asked in surprise. "You are a smart elephant!"

He climbed down the elephant's trunk. He stroked the elephant's tree-like leg and said, "You're my friend. I'll call you Haatee."

The elephant raised his trunk and sounded, "Ahoo!"

"See you tomorrow!" Viku called, as his new friend turned and disappeared into the forest.

The next morning, as soon as Viku woke up, he hurried into the forest, hoping to meet the elephant. Haatee was waiting near the river. Viku joyfully ran to him. The elephant lowered his trunk so Viku could climb on his back. Then Haatee ambled into the forest.

The sun's rays glistened through the branches. The tropical forest looked bright and green, and a damp, woodsy fragrance rose from the ground. Birds chirped in high branches, and long-tailed monkeys jumped from tree to tree.

Viku remained silent for some time. Then he told Haatee, "My parents walked ten miles yesterday, but couldn't find any work. So we had nothing to eat except for the few bananas I brought home. I hope they find work today."

Haatee plodded on quietly. After some time, Viku saw that they were going in a different direction. There was no elephant path like the one he had seen the day before.

"Where are you taking me today?" he asked. But the elephant made no sound, nor gave him any sign.

After a long time, they came out of the forest and onto a

hilly road. In the distance Viku saw a green stretch of land with water around it.

Haatee stopped at the water's edge. Viku jumped down, but did not know why they had come to this place.

The elephant pointed his trunk at the grove of trees. Viku waded through the shallow water and entered the grove. He saw a clearing.

Heaps of elephant tusks and bones were scattered everywhere. He realized Haatee had brought him to the elephants' graveyard.

Viku had heard of this place, but no one he knew had ever seen an elephants' graveyard. He looked around. Yes, there were signs that many elephants had died in this place. Viku remembered his grandfather telling him about elephants' graveyards. When an elephant grows old and knows his time has come, he says goodbye to his family and friends and goes there. It is a sacred place for elephants. Once they come to the graveyard, they eat little or nothing and stay there until they die.

Viku understood why Haatee would not enter the grove. One day Haatee would come here and not leave. Viku saw many beautiful tusks, some more than four feet long. Selling a tusk to the ivory carvers in town would make his family very rich. But he could not take any. He felt it would be stealing. Viku trudged out of the graveyard.

When the elephant saw Viku come out empty-handed, he again pointed his trunk at the grove.

Viku went back and selected a small tusk that was smooth and beautiful. He then folded his hands, bowed his head and said quietly, "Thank you for this gift."

Haatee brought him back to the river. Viku stroked Haatee's trunk and said, "Thank you, Haatee. You are a good friend. I'll see you tomorrow."

The ivory tusk astonished Viku's parents. They didn't know what to make of his story, but they believed him because he never told lies. The next day, his father took the tusk to town and sold it for a large sum of money. He did not walk home that day, but came back on a cart drawn by two large oxen.

Rice, lentils, sugar and other food items filled the cart. He even bought nice clothes for the whole family and a special brown vest for Viku, embroidered with little animals. It was the kind that *mahuts*, the elephant drivers, wear in India.

Viku went to the forest every day to play with Haatee, his elephant friend. Haatee always lifted him up with his trunk and put him on his back. Then they explored many places in the jungle. Sometimes Viku took Haatee to the river and splashed water on him; Haatee enjoyed that very much. They became very good friends.

One morning Viku saw a police van in front of their hut. A policeman with a large, olive-green hat was talking to his father.

"Someone from here sold an elephant tusk," the policeman said. "Do you know anything about it?"

"I am the one who sold it," Viku's father replied.

"Did you know it's illegal to kill an elephant?" The policeman glared at Viku's father.

"But I didn't kill an elephant. My son got it from his friend."

"Really!" exclaimed the policeman. "Tell me about this friend." His voice was stern. "Don't lie to me or I'll put you in jail."

Viku ran outside. "Haatee took me to a place where there were many tusks," he told the policeman excitedly. "I took only a small one that I could carry."

"Haatee is an elephant," his father told the policeman. "He has become Viku's friend because Viku saved him from a snake."

"I'm not here to listen to crazy stories," the policeman snarled. "I'll give you three days to tell me how you got the tusk, or I'll throw you in jail."

"It's true!" Viku told the policeman. "My friend Haatee gave me the tusk."

However, the policeman stormed away, saying, "I shall be back in three days!"

Viku's mother saw and heard the policeman from the kitchen. Her face became pale. She knew the police did not treat poor people like them nicely. Sometimes the police beat them for no reason. She did not know how she could help her husband, or where to go for help. She started to cry silently.

Viku went out to play with Haatee, but his mind could not stay still. He was afraid of the policeman and he was worried about his father. What would happen if the policeman took his father to jail? He didn't even know where the jail was. He was not old enough or strong enough to work. How would they survive?

He did not kill an elephant to get the tusk. But how could he convince the police?

He splashed river water on Haatee and told him what had happened. He didn't know if Haatee understood his fear of losing his father, but it felt good to tell his friend.

After three days, the policeman returned. This time he brought two more policemen with him. "How did you get the tusk?" he asked Viku's father again. "Tell me the truth."

"My son found the tusk in the elephants' graveyard," Viku's father told him.

The policeman didn't like hearing the same story again. "Well, does the elephant visit your house, too?" he jeered at Viku's father.

"No. I haven't seen the elephant."

The policeman then asked Viku, "If your story is true, can you take me to the elephants' graveyard?"

"The elephant took me to the place," Viku told the policeman. "It's far away. I don't know how to get there by myself. I only know it is inside a small grove of trees surrounded by shallow water."

"You are both lying," the policeman snarled in a gruff voice. "Tell your story to the judge and see what happens to you."

The policeman ordered his men to handcuff Viku's father and take him away.

Viku's mother wailed. Viku didn't know what to do.

While the policeman was questioning Viku's father, a crowd gathered in front of the hut. Just as the policeman started the van to take Viku's father away, people in the crowd began murmuring and pointing toward the forest. An elephant was coming! Elephants rarely came near the village, so the sight of the elephant created great excitement.

Viku shouted, "That's my friend, Haatee!"

The elephant marched to Viku and stood in front of the police car. Then he took a small tusk from behind his ear and laid it on the ground.

Viku exclaimed, "See! See! He brought me another present!"

The policeman freed Viku's father and left the village, mumbling, "I saw it myself, but I don't believe it!"

Viku and the Elephant

Part 2

Viku was very happy. His parents didn't have to search for work anymore. His father spent his time fishing, and his mother stayed home and happily cooked sweets for him. He played with Haatee every day in the forest.

One day his father said, "You love animals so much, Viku. How would you like to visit the zoo tomorrow?"

Viku beamed with joy. "Yes! Yes!" he cried, and he ran out to tell Haatee.

He explained to Haatee what a zoo was and that one could see many animals there. He described some animals he had heard of but never seen. "The zoo brings them from many countries," he told his friend. "They aren't free, but zookeepers feed them. They don't have to search for food."

Viku was excited, but he found that Haatee did not share his enthusiasm. Haatee looked away from him and gave a sad cry, "Ouhooo!"

"I shall tell you all about the zoo when I come back," Viku promised.

Viku and his father went by train to the big zoo in Calcutta. This was Viku's first train ride. He wore his new vest and wished Haatee were with him.

The zoo was crowded. Children and their families rushed from place to place, looking at the animals. Viku visited the white tigers, the rhinoceros with one horn, and the snake house.

He had never seen so many different snakes! Cobras, pythons, vipers, sea snakes, and even one that looked like a green vine hanging down from a branch.

After lunch, Viku saw people running and scrambling about. A man shouted, "A mad elephant has broken out of his cage! Run away!" Some ran into nearby buildings for safety, some climbed trees, and some just rushed here and there. No one seemed to know what to do.

Suddenly, the elephant appeared on the road with broken chains around his legs. He swung his trunk from side to side. The elephant looked angry, but Viku saw that his eyes were sad.

Then a van came from the opposite direction. Several guards jumped out and formed a line with their rifles aimed at the elephant.

Were they going to shoot the elephant? Viku's heart started to beat hard. He ran into the middle of the road and walked cautiously toward the elephant.

"Get away," people shouted to him. "It's a mad elephant!"

Viku did not listen to them and stepped forward. When he came close to the elephant, he cupped his hands around his mouth and trumpeted, "Ahoo! Ahoo!" It was the same sound his friend, Haatee, made in the forest.

The elephant stopped when he heard the sound from Viku. His trunk stood still. Viku bellowed again, "Ahoo! Ahoo!"

The elephant walked slowly toward Viku. The guards yelled at him, "Move out of the way! We're going to shoot him!"

But Viku did not move, and the elephant came to him. Viku touched the elephant's leg and talked to him as if the elephant were his friend. The elephant picked him up and put him on his back.

Viku told the people the elephant wouldn't hurt anyone. "He only wants to go back to his home in the forest."

The elephant, with Viku on his back, walked along the road that circled the zoo. The visitors followed them. More and more people joined in, and soon they formed a large procession. The crowd was jovial and cheered for Viku and the elephant.

Newspaper reporters came and took many pictures of them. The guards went to the director of the zoo and told him about the enormous crowd following Viku and the elephant. The director came out of his office.

Viku told the director that if he promised to release the elephant in the forest, the elephant wouldn't be angry anymore.

The crowd began to shout, "Yes! Yes! Take him back to his forest!"

The director had no choice and agreed. Then he stared at Viku, saying, "I don't know which forest he came from."

"He looks like my friend, Haatee," Viku told him. "Take him to the Shapnobahn Forest."

Viku and his father returned home late that night. Viku couldn't wait to tell Haatee what had happened at the zoo.

Many villagers came to greet him. They had heard on the radio how he did not let the guards kill the zoo elephant. They were happy and gave him home-cooked sweets.

The next day, newspapers printed his picture on the front page, showing him riding the zoo elephant. The words above the picture said: "The Boy Who Understands Elephants!" The papers described how Viku bravely saved the elephant.

One newspaper reporter came all the way from the city to Viku's village and asked him many questions. The reporter then wrote a long story about Viku: how he became the friend of an elephant in the Shapnobahn forest, the secret elephant path he had seen, and about the elephants' graveyard. The reporter also wrote that if someone discovered the place where Viku found tusks, the finder would become very rich.

Viku and the Elephant

Part 3

One sunny afternoon when Viku was playing with Haatee, several men carrying long rifles suddenly surrounded them. A rough man with curly hair, a big mustache, and bushy eyebrows told Viku, "Come with us or we'll shoot the elephant." That man was the leader.

They were strangers with guns, but they were not hunting. Viku's heart sank. He had a feeling that they were up to no good. He did not want his friend to get hurt, so he told Haatee to go home. But instead, Haatee walked a little distance away and hid out of sight.

The men tied Viku's hands and took him to their camp in the forest. Two large tents and many people were there. They all had rifles.

"You see we have big guns," the bandit leader told Viku. "We can kill the elephant. You don't want that, do you?"

"No. Please, please don't hurt him!"

"Then tell your friend to take us to the graveyard. We only want a few tusks. We won't harm him."

"That's their sacred place," Viku said. "You mustn't go there!"

The bandit leader laughed. "If he doesn't take us there, we'll shoot him." He put his hands around Viku's neck and said, "And then we will take care of you!" His eyes burned with rage.

Viku realized they were ivory thieves. They would steal the tusks and destroy the sacred place of the elephants. He also knew they would hurt Haatee if he didn't do what they wanted.

"Will you leave us alone if my friend shows you where the graveyard is?" he asked the leader.

"Yes."

"Then take me to the river in the morning. I'll ask my friend."

"That's a good boy," the leader said.

When Viku didn't return home in the evening, his parents started to worry. This had never happened before. They knew he had gone to play with Haatee. Had Haatee taken him somewhere far away?

Viku's father held his *hukka-pipe* and stared at the forest without smoking. Viku's mother paced between the kitchen and the bedroom, folding and refolding her son's shirts and pants.

The sun dipped over the horizon of the vast forest. Birds returned to their nests in the trees, their chatter filling the air. Normally it was a soothing sound at the end of the day, but today their twitter disturbed Viku's father. This was a dangerous time in the forest, when hungry animals look for their last meal. He thought of tigers on land, and crocodiles in the river. Shapnobahn forest had many man-eating tigers. Every year they killed woodcutters and fishermen. And the big crocodiles would eat almost anything!

"We should have given him a mask," Viku's mother said.

Viku's father nodded. He had not yet told Viku about the mask. A tiger won't attack a man who faces it, so wearing a mask on the back of one's head fools tigers. "I shall teach him to tie a mask," he told her.

"He must also learn to read the signs of crocodiles in the river," she murmured. "They move so quietly, and attack so suddenly."

Soon the birds quieted down and darkness came. Viku's father paced in front of the hut. He didn't know what to do. No one could enter the forest at this time. Besides, where would they go to look for Viku? He could be anywhere.

Viku's mother put red and white flowers on the family altar and sat down in front of it. She prayed to save her son. Her vision blurred with tears. "Oh, my Viku!" She started to cry. "Where are you, my son?"

She turned up the wick of the earthen lamp on the altar. Then she took a banana leaf and bent it into the shape of a boat and stitched it with sticks. She put flowers from the altar into the boat. She searched the house, found a small candle, and placed it inside.

"Let's go to the river," she told her husband. "The river goddess will help us."

Viku's parents walked to the river. They could barely see the stream in the dark, but the flowing sound comforted them.

Viku's mother lit the candle and let the boat float in the stream. She said a prayer with folded hands. Viku's father prayed silently.

The leaf boat moved swiftly down the stream. The flowers in the boat looked very pretty under the candlelight. The two gazed at the boat as it floated away in the distance.

In the morning, the ivory thieves took Viku to the river, where Haatee was waiting. Viku explained to his friend with signs and words that these men wanted to go to the graveyard, and that they would kill them both if Haatee didn't show the way. He then mimicked the sad sound Haatee made when the snake was biting him: "Ouhooo! Ouhooo!"

The thieves didn't know what Viku was doing. Haatee swung his trunk gently back and forth, as if thinking it over. Finally, he sounded, "Ahoo!"

Viku told the leader that his friend would show them the path to the graveyard, but it was far away.

The leader didn't want everyone in the camp to know the location of the graveyard, so he asked only his assistant and one guard to come with him.

The three men followed Haatee with Viku on his back. Viku saw that Haatee walked along a new path. It wasn't the path he remembered from before when Haatee took him to the graveyard. That path was not flat like this one, and he couldn't see a green patch of land surrounded by water in the distance. But he did not say anything.

They passed several streams. Viku could see many mangrove trees lining the banks. They entered a dark and tangled part of the forest. Viku realized the elephant was going south, where the streams were full of crocodiles.

"How much farther?" the leader asked Viku after several hours of hiking.

"The graveyard is still far away," Viku replied. "We could rest now and start fresh in the morning."

The leader stopped walking. "My two men are very tired," he said.

The guard and the assistant pitched a tent.

The leader shook his finger in front of Viku's nose, saying, "Remember, I'll shoot the elephant if you try to run away at night."

Soon it became pitch dark, and they heard many animal cries. Sometimes it sounded as if the animals were very near, and might jump on them at any moment. The leader and his assistant saw two glowing lights in the distance. Viku told them, "Those are eyes of a Royal Bengal tiger—they glow at night." Terrified, the three men couldn't sleep.

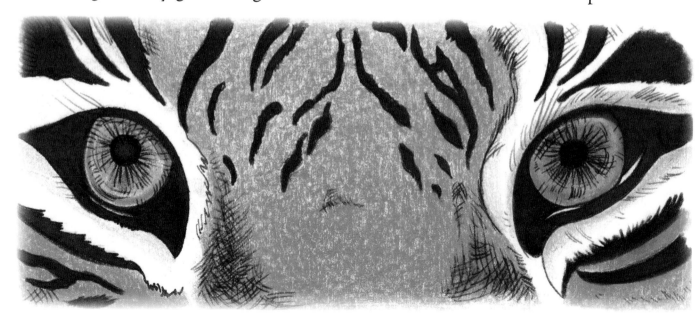

When daylight came, the leader told the guard to fetch water from the river to make tea. The man went out, but soon they all heard his cries for help. Viku, the leader, and his assistant rushed to the river and saw a crocodile dragging the man underwater.

He struggled to free himself, but it was all over within a minute. The rapid churning stopped and the water calmed; the river flowed on as if nothing had happened.

"Stupid man!" the leader announced without pity. "Didn't he know the river is full of crocodiles?"

"Completely stupid," his assistant echoed.

"Let's get out of here," the leader growled. "We must get to the graveyard today."

Viku climbed on top of Haatee and they resumed their journey. The forest looked beautiful in the morning light, but the leader and his assistant didn't see the lovely green trees and plants or hear the sweet twittering of the birds. They were hungry and tired, and they dragged their feet as they walked.

When the sun rose above the trees, they saw monkeys lined up on the bank of the river, watching something. Viku noticed that it was a small banana-leaf boat drifting in the water.

"A leaf-boat for the river goddess," he said softly. The red and magenta flowers inside the green leaf looked very pleasing in the soft sunlight. Viku thought of his mother and felt sad. He wondered if she had sent the boat.

"Is there food in the boat?" the leader asked Viku.

"That's an offering for the river goddess," Viku said.

The leader did not care and threw a stone at the leaf boat, but the stone only reached as far as the monkeys.

"Uh! Uh! Uh!" the monkeys hooted and turned to the stone-thrower. They began to gather into a gang. That frightened the leader. He moved closer to Haatee. "Faster, faster!" he commanded the elephant, though he himself was too weary to move any faster.

After two more hours of walking, they emerged from the deep forest. Here, the river spread out and broke into streams before meeting the ocean. The soil that the river brought down from the mountains formed small islands in the area. Haatee stopped walking and Viku pointed his finger toward a beautiful view. There in the distance was a green patch of land surrounded by water.

"It's exactly what I read in the newspaper!" the leader said. "The elephant has finally brought us to the right place!" A smile spread over his face.

Viku knew it was not the graveyard. But the two men, being very tired from worrying about tigers all night and the long walk through the hot jungle, thought they had reached the elephants' graveyard. They wanted to go to the island right away, but the crocodiles in the water frightened them. They didn't want to die like the guard.

"You know crocodiles never attack elephants," the leader said to Viku. "Your friend can carry us to the island. Get down and tell him to take us there."

As soon as the leader and his assistant climbed onto Haatee's back, Haatee started to wade through the water.

The two men couldn't sit still on the elephant's back. They were too excited by greed. When Haatee reached the island, they jumped down and ran into the thicket of bushes and small trees that grew there. Haatee turned around and waded swiftly back through the water to Viku.

The two men came out of the bushes a few minutes later and shouted to Viku, "There are no tusks here! It's full of silt and sand. Nothing, nothing is here! You brought us to the wrong place. Take us back!"

Haatee trumpeted, "Ahoo! Ahoo!"

Viku called to the two men, "My friend says you'll soon find the path to the graveyard."

The leader fired a shot at Viku and missed him. He was too far away. But the sound of the rifle caught the attention of the crocodiles. Several large ones crawled out of the water and lined up on the shore of the tiny island. They had huge, triangular jaws full of dagger-like teeth.

Viku saw that the bandits could not escape from the island. He climbed on top of his friend, and they headed back home.

He patted Haatee's ears and smiled. "What a smart, smart elephant you are."

45

THE END

Foreign Words & Pronunciation Guide

Ahoo (Aaa-hooo)   A cheerful sound made by an elephant

Bodhi (Bo-dhi) tree   A large tree common in India

Gurkha (Goor-khaa)   Word used for the people or things from Nepal

Haatee (Haa-tee)   Word for elephant in India

Hukka (Hook-ka)   A smoking pipe

Mahut (Maa-hoot)   An elephant driver in India

Ouhooo (Ow-hoooo)   A long, sad cry of an elephant

Shapnobahn (Shop-no-bahn)   Dream forest

Viku (Vee-ku)   A boy's name from India

Discussion Questions

1. Would you like Viku as a friend? Why?

2. Would you like Haatee as a friend? Why?

3. What did Viku do that shows he is a good person?

4. Do you think elephant's graveyards exist?

5. Why is the elephant's graveyard special to Haatee and Viku?

6. Why didn't Viku ask his friend to bring more tusks for him?

7. Did Viku ever take advantage of his friendship with Haatee?

8. Do animals like living in the zoo?

9. Name some animals in India.

10. Name some tropical trees.

11. How do tiger masks help a person in the forest?

12. Why did Viku's mother launch a flower boat?

13. How did the bandits come to know about the elephant's graveyard?

14. Did the Bandit leader bully Viku? What would you have done?

15. What do you think happened after Viku returned home?

16. Can you imagine a different ending for the story?

Author

Born in Calcutta, India, Debu Majumdar came to the U.S. in 1964 to do graduate work and received a doctorate degree in physics.

His first book, a collection of creative non-fiction essays, *From the Ganges to the Snake River*, was first published by Idaho State University and then by Caxton Press; it interweaves Indian culture with North-West American reality. He currently writes Op-Ed Columns for two Idaho newspapers. He lives with his wife in Idaho Falls, Idaho.

Illustrator

Lynn Wolfe is a college freshman and freelance artist and writer. She illustrated Viku and the Elephant during high school.

Among several awards, she received a Certificate of Special Congressional Recognition in 2007. She lives in southern California.

Praise by National Award Winning Teachers and Others

"*Viku and the Elephant* is a wonderful story that can teach us all about the importance of friendship and doing the right thing. The special bond between Viku and Haatee is really what drew me into this story. I also appreciate how this story exposes students to India and the Indian culture. This story would be great to use with students to cover comprehension strategies such as cause and effect, problem/solution, and author's purpose."
  - Martin Martinez, Milken Educator Award (2010), Gresham, Oregon

"Students need to be culturally diverse and expand their horizons. *Viku and the Elephant* is an extraordinary story of the adventures of a boy and his great big friend. I was on the edge of my seat and it left me wanting to read more. The vivid details tell the story like it is ...the culture in the story is well kept. ...wonderful work in educating our children."
  -Rogelio Garcia, Milken Educator Award (2010), Dallas, Texas.

"The story gives all readers, young and old, a glimpse into the cultural values and hardships of an impoverished Indian boy. ...I think students could learn a great deal comparing their lives to Viku's and by discussing the decisions Viku makes in the story."
  -Joel Robins, Milken Educator Award (2010), Chesapeake, Virginia

"*Viku and the Elephant*' by Debu Majumdar weaves beautifully written details and vibrant visuals ...it is well paced, engaging, and easy to read. The reader is rewarded with a glimpse of another culture, and it offers children the opportunity to expand vocabulary and embrace cultural connections. ... it would be an excellent book to use in K-5 reading. ...the illustrations were very vivid and added to the story."
  -Kathie J. Heusel, Milken Educator Award (2008), Great Falls, Montana

"A very entertaining and informational story. Debu not only tells an enchanting story of a boy, his family and a pet elephant but he also teaches Indian culture. The illustrations are very vivid and colorful. While I teach middle school - this story will be beneficial for examples of writing style and voice. A must read for all elementary classes."
  -Mikki Samargis-Nuckols, Milken Educator Award (2007), Idaho Falls, Idaho

"…I enjoyed the relationship between the boy and the elephant. I think it has a deep underlying tone about how friends work with each other in unusual ways. …The pictures were gorgeous!"

-Jennifer Smith, Milken Educator Award (2006), Twentynine Palms, California.

"*Viku and the Elephant* would make an excellent addition to an elementary classroom's multicultural library. …provides an opportunity for teachers to engage their students in discussion of culturally-sacred issues vs. for-profit issues."

-Sharon Moser, Ph.D., Milken Educator Award (2004), Frostproof, Florida.

"I have never been to India, but Debu Majumdar transported me there through the adventures of a boy. … easy to read story that children of all ages will surely learn from and enjoy. Lynn Wolf's illustrations tie the story together with color and beautiful art that helps draw the reader into the story."

-Chris Wilmes, Milken Educator Award (2006), Idaho Falls, Idaho

"…enough suspense and action to keep the attention of the children who are just beginning to take on the complexities of longer and more challenging chapter books. …The story gives the reader a chance to vicariously fulfill a dream that a fair number of children might have. Who wouldn't love to have an elephant for a best friend, who lowers his trunk down specifically so you can climb up and ride around on him? And who listens to you, the child, and not the grown-ups! Whereas Horton, Dumbo, and Babar (lovable as they may be) are elephants one might want to befriend, one does not encounter them in their natural habitats. This heightens the vicarious experience of the reader.

-Susan Seefeldt, Youth Services Department, Fairbanks North Star Borough Public Library, Fairbanks, Alaska.

Made in the USA
Charleston, SC
28 April 2011